The Pencil

We have to take care of our belongings. If we don't, we may need to ask other people for help. Married couples should also help each other. This book is dedicated to my children, grandchildren, and great-grandchildren. —SA

For Jayco and Alex; may you always be resourceful. —MV

Published by Inhabit Media Inc. | www.inhabitmedia.com

Inhabit Media Inc. (Iqaluit) P.O. Box 11125, Iqaluit, Nunavut, X0A 1H0
(Toronto) 191 Eglinton Avenue East, Suite 310, Toronto, Ontario, M4P 1K1

Editors: Neil Christopher and Kathleen Keenan
Art director: Danny Christopher
Designer: Astrid Arijanto

We acknowledge the support of the Canada Council for the Arts for our publishing program. This project was made possible in part by the Government of Canada.

ISBN: 978-1-77227-216-1

Printed in Canada

Library and Archives Canada Cataloguing in Publication

Avingaq, Susan, author
    The pencil / by Susan Avingaq and Maren Vsetula ; illustrated by
Charlene Chua.

ISBN 978-1-77227-216-1 (hardcover)

    I. Vsetula, Maren, 1979-, author II. Chua, Charlene, illustrator III. Title.

PS8601.V58P46 2019   jC813'.6   C2018-905984-2

The Pencil

by Susan Avingaq and Maren Vsetula

illustrated by Charlene Chua

"See you later!" *Anaana* said. "You three be good for *Ataata*."

"We will!" Rebecca, Peter, and I said in unison.

The warm air rushed out of the *iglu* as our mother left to go help a woman in a neighbouring iglu deliver a baby.

As Anaana passed our lead dog, Qanukia, we heard him let out a little yip. He loved attention!

Our iglu was a very cozy place. We didn't have much, so our parents told us to use what we had wisely.

My favourite place in our iglu was the corner near the *qulliq*, where Anaana kept her important things in a wooden box. This is where she kept things like tools for cleaning skins, needles and sinew for sewing, and even a pencil!

"The sun's out!" Ataata said. "Why don't you draw on the window?"

8

Anaana had been teaching my older
sister and me how to write by letting
us practise on the ice window. Rebecca and I loved
writing with our fingers on the frosty surface.

We also liked to watch Anaana write letters to people in other camps with the pencil. It was so neat! Because we didn't always have paper, she would use wrappers and other things, like the tea box or the sugar bag.

But now, we were all alone with Ataata, so we could not watch Anaana write letters. It was nice to spend some time with Ataata. Sometimes he even let us do things that Anaana didn't let us do . . .

At first, we played all our regular games.

We had a jumping contest on the floor of the iglu. Then, we played with the dolls that *Anaanatsiaq* had made for us.

We even played a game of hide-and-seek with a blindfold. But soon, we got tired of all our regular games, and Anaana was still not back.

Peter was beginning to get restless. "What else can we do?" he asked.

I knew something that would be really fun to do: using the pencil. We could never ask Ataata that because the pencil was so special to Anaana. Oh, but it would be so much fun!

As we were thinking of what else we could do, Ataata did something that he almost never did—he went into Anaana's things and pulled out the pencil!

"The pencil, the pencil!" Peter and I yelled.
We hardly ever got to see it. It got a
little bit smaller every time we saw it.

It was very short now, with only a tiny
little bit of eraser left. Ataata passed
me the pencil, saying, "How about
drawing some pictures for your
brother?"

I couldn't believe it! Anaana always said that we needed to be very careful with the pencil and that it wasn't a toy.

I took the pencil. I was a little nervous, but I loved how it felt in my hand. Ataata pulled out a piece of paper for me to draw on. I knew it was the only piece of paper we had.

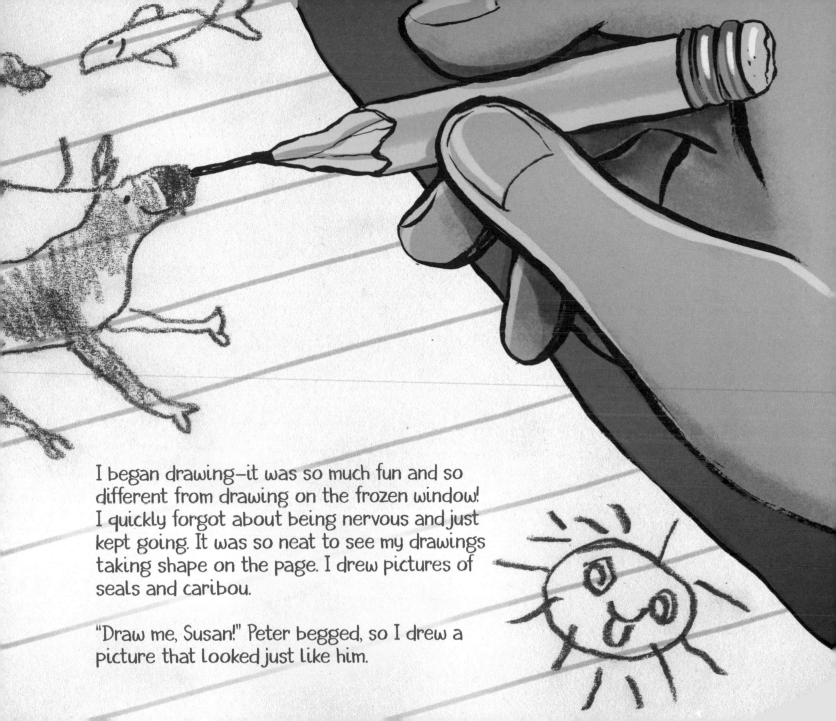

I began drawing—it was so much fun and so
different from drawing on the frozen window!
I quickly forgot about being nervous and just
kept going. It was so neat to see my drawings
taking shape on the page. I drew pictures of
seals and caribou.

"Draw me, Susan!" Peter begged, so I drew a
picture that looked just like him.

As the time passed, we each got a turn to use the pencil. When we had filled up the sheet of paper, Ataata pulled out part of an old tea box. Rebecca practised her writing, Peter drew scribbles, and even Ataata drew some different types of *inuksuit* for us to learn about.

Ataata had to sharpen the pencil a few times with his knife. It was getting shorter and shorter, and I was beginning to worry about how Anaana would react when she came home.

Just as we finished drawing all over the tea box, I heard Qanukia
let out an excited yip. Anaana was back! I wondered what she would
say when she saw the tiny pencil and our only piece of paper full of
drawings.

Anaana looked tired. She was happy that the new baby had been born,
but when she saw that the pencil had been taken out, and that it was
even smaller now, the smile on her face faded.

"Look what we did, Anaana!" Peter yelled in excitement.

"Wow," Anaana said slowly, looking at all our drawings. "You have all been very busy!"

"Did you see my drawing of Peter? Look, Anaana!" I was so proud that I wanted to make sure she saw that one.

"I see," Anaana said. "You know, the reason we have to use our things very wisely is because they are quite difficult to get. We have only one pencil right now, and we won't be able to get another until we return to the trading post," she said.

We all must have looked a little disappointed. Anaana saw our faces and smiled.

"I'm happy you had a great day with the pencil," Anaana said. "And this drawing really does look like Peter!"

We crowded around Anaana, pointing out all the drawings we had done.

It's amazing how something as small as a pencil brought us so much joy that day! I would always remember what Anaana had said about using things wisely. And I knew that even though we didn't have much, we always took care of what we did have.

Glossary

Anaana (a-naa-na): The Inuktitut word for "mother."

Anaanatsiaq (a-na-nat-see-ak): The Inuktitut word for "grandmother."

Ataata (a-taa-ta): The Inuktitut word for "father."

iglu (ee-glue): The Inuktitut word for a dome-shaped house made with blocks of snow.

inuksuit (in-uk-su-eet): The Inuktitut word for traditional Inuit stone markers.

qulliq (kood-lick): The Inuktitut word for an oil-burning lamp.

Contributors

Susan Avingaq was born on the land and moved to the community of Igloolik, Nunavut, in 1967. She loves to go camping and fishing whenever she can and often brings new people along to teach them these land skills. She enjoys sewing and teaching younger people important cultural practices. She is an extremely resourceful person and thinks that this is an important quality to pass on to the younger generation. She has many grandchildren, with whom she likes to share her stories. Her previous picture book, *Fishing with Grandma*, was published in 2016.

Maren Vsetula is a teacher. She loves to spend as much time on the land as she can, camping, hiking, paddling, and dogsledding. She has lived and worked in Nunavut for over a decade. She is the co-author of *Fishing with Grandma*.

Charlene Chua picked up her first pencil when she around three years old and never really put it down. She now creates illustrations using her trusty pencils, as well as brushes, paints, inks, and computers. She also has way, way too many erasers. Charlene lives in Hamilton, Ontario, with her husband and their two cats.